Homework on Pluto

By Lou Treleaven

Why not visit... PLUTO?

This year, why not bypass the exciting attractions of **Jupiter** and **Saturn** and keep going for seven and a half billion kilometres until you get to **Pluto**?

"But it's too small!"

Pluto may be small, but that means you can see everything on the planet in just a few days, giving you plenty of time for the week's journey home again.

The **7** Wonders of PLUTO

☑ Glowing Canyon
☑ Blue Prairies
☒ Pulsating Swamp
☑ Skwitch dance
☐ President's front garden
☐ Erm...

"But it's too smelly!"

Don't worry, the President of Pluto has sprayed the whole planet with Vom-Be-Gone so all the smelly vomblefruit trees have been killed. Well, nearly all.

"It's too far away!"

Think of the journey as part of the holiday. Or why not sleep? Solitaire can also be a fun game.

OH GO ON, COME TO PLUTO.
PLEASE?

Max 26C, min 9C   10th Grylls 2317   1 plound

SKWITCH SNATCH

A number of handbags have been snatched in Dome 1 recently and the culprits have one thing in common – they are birds! "Skwitches are attracted by strong smells and bright colours," Dome 1's skwitch herder explains. She recommends carrying a dull-coloured handbag. "Beige or taupe are particularly boring colours that definitely won't attract skwitches."

VOMBLEFRUIT TREE STILL GROWING!

Pluto's only vomblefruit tree is still shooting up, thanks to the efforts of Jon Fisher from Earth and Straxi Dooly from Pluto. The young pen-pals saved life on Pluto by keeping the last vomblefruit seed safe when all the rest of the smelly trees had been destroyed. "I only sent the seed to Jon as a joke," Straxi told us, "but when I realised everything on Pluto was dying without the trees, I told Jon and he had the idea of sending the seed back. It came with a police escort and everything!" While all of Pluto waits for the tree to grow, no one is more eager than the blue-headed skwitches. Our giant native birds just love vomblefruit, but they'll have to be patient. Fruit won't grow on the tree for a few more months yet. Let's hope it's not too smelly!

LIGHTEN UP

The President has apologised for the bad sunsets again this week. "The dome lights are still playing up," he told us. "I must particularly apologise for Thursday's sunset with clashing colours and a persistent flicker that gave several residents a migraine." The President promises a fantastic display at the weekend, and asks that residents please use smaller pieces of paper for their complaints postbox has burst.

GOT A HEAD FOR HEIGHTS?

Why not stay at the Vertigo Hotel? It's built for tourists, so you'll have the whole place to yourself!

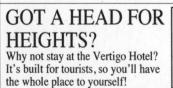

6

Class 5H

Northcroft School

England

Earth

Dear Jon,

This is a very proud moment. A pupil of mine from 5H, going to Pluto! I'm sure you will want to keep up your writing skills while you are away, so why don't you write to me and the class about your trip? I look forward to hearing from you.

Best wishes,

Mrs Hall

Class 5H

Northcroft School

England

Earth

Tuesday 18 July 2317

Dear Jon,

I have not received your letter telling me all about
your flight. Please write to me and 5H using lots of
describing words.

Keep it short will you?
Rex Smith

You should not write on other people's letters, Rex.
But well done for not making any spelling mistakes.

Best wishes,

Mrs Hall

Class 5H

Northcroft School

England

Earth

Dear Jon,

May I remind you that you have only been given

permission to go to Pluto if you can keep up with your

school work. If you do not wish to write to the class

about your holiday, I can easily send you some maths

to do. Today we are studying algebra.

Best wishes,

Mrs Hall

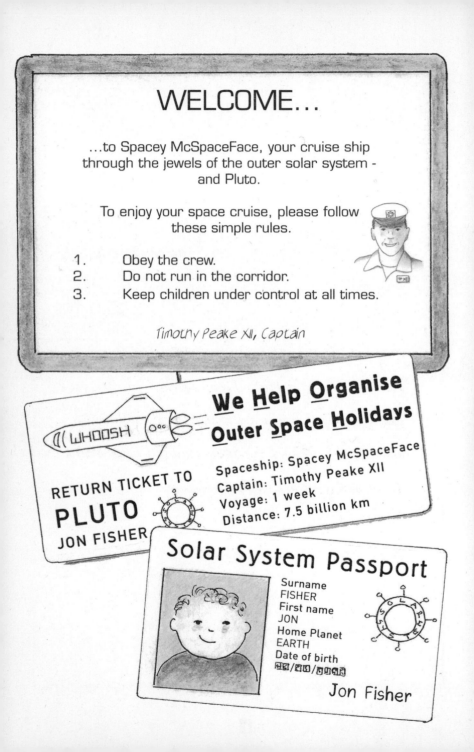

WELCOME...

...to Spacey McSpaceFace, your cruise ship through the jewels of the outer solar system - and Pluto.

To enjoy your space cruise, please follow these simple rules.

1. Obey the crew.
2. Do not run in the corridor.
3. Keep children under control at all times.

Timothy Peake XII, Captain

We Help Organise Outer Space Holidays

((WHOOSH

RETURN TICKET TO
PLUTO
JON FISHER

Spaceship: Spacey McSpaceFace
Captain: Timothy Peake XII
Voyage: 1 week
Distance: 7.5 billion km

Solar System Passport

Surname
FISHER
First name
JON
Home Planet
EARTH
Date of birth

Jon Fisher

me

Vertigo Hotel

Dome 1

Pluto

Pluto dates!!!

→ Fiveday 28 Grylls 2317

Dear Mrs Hall and 5H,

The journey to Pluto was brilliant. I saw Jupiter, Saturn, Uranus and Neptune on the way. I didn't see Mars as my big brother had me in a headlock. Jupiter was my favourite. Dad said it is a gas giant, so a bit like big bruv when he has too many baked beans.

It took eight days to get to Pluto, as we had to stop at all the other planets on the way. Big bruv spent most of the time chasing me up and down the corridors. Little sis spent most of the time galloping around being My Ickle Pickle Dress Up Princess Pony.

Mum watered the plants on the ship, even when they didn't want to be watered. That's what she does in her job at Dawn's Lawns.

Dad 'improved' the ship's computers
because he likes taking things
apart for fun. This
meant we got stuck in
orbit around Jupiter
which added an extra day
to the journey.

The Captain was not
pleased.

It was just like home only
bigger and surrounded by space. But
it all stopped when big bruv chased
me into the cockpit and I fell right
onto the controls. The Captain

swerved and said a

rude word. Mum

made us all

apologise, but I

pointed out that the

Captain only

NEARLY crashed into Saturn, which

isn't the same as actually doing it.

Plus he said the rude word, which is

worse.

Dad offered to take the control panel

apart and put it back together but

the Captain didn't look too happy

about that. Mum said she couldn't

take us anywhere, not even into deep
space, and maybe she should ask the
Captain to turn around and go home.
The Captain didn't look too happy
about that either and said the sooner
he dropped us off at Pluto the better.

Mum has just read this letter and
says I haven't used enough describing
words, so I asked her how she would
describe the journey.

Long, she said. Very long.

From Jon

WELCOME (AGAIN)

To Spacey McSpaceFace, your cruise ship through the jewels of the outer solar system - and Pluto.

To enjoy your cruise, please follow these NEW <u>AMENDED</u> rules.

1. Do not gallop in the corridor pretending to be a space dinosaur.

2. Do not enter the cockpit pretending to be a space dinosaur.

3. Do not attempt to 'mend' the cockpit because you like taking things apart for fun.

4. Just stay away from the cockpit altogether.

Timothy Peake XII, Captain

Class 5H

Northcroft School

England

Earth

Dear Jon,

Thank you for your letter which I finally received today. I have had a wonderful idea! When we go back to school in September we will do a class project on Pluto! So for your holiday homework please could you write a page for me about Pluto's landscape and send it with your next letter.

Best wishes,

Mrs Hall

Vertigo Hotel

Dome 1

Pluto

Fiveday 4 Armstrong 237

Dear Mrs Hall,

We have finally got to Pluto and it is
amazing! Everyone lives in domes so
they can breathe and Dome 1 is the
biggest.

We went through a giant airlock
and into the Shuttleport and
there were crowds of
people waiting.

Lots of them had strange hairstyles and shoes because they don't have fashions here so you can look as weird as you want. Big bruv fitted in well.

I looked for my penpal Straxi but I couldn't see her and then a little group came up and one of them was the President of Pluto.

He had a special ~~medlai~~ medallion with President written on it so everyone knew who he was and a baseball cap and a beard. And Gran was with him as she has been visiting Pluto on her planet-hopping trip and has got to know everyone really well, especially the President who she calls 'poppet' and 'honeybun' which is a bit strange as he doesn't look like a honeybun to me.

Straxi was standing next to Gran and we finally met after writing all those letters. We grinned and suddenly I didn't know what to say. "I wish I could just write hello on a piece of paper," I said,

and she laughed and Gran gave me a
hug and everybody cheered. "Pleased
to meet you at last, Jon," the
President said. "You and Straxi have
saved life on Pluto."

And I blushed and felt secretly
pleased because we have! Straxi had
sent me a vomblefruit as a joke, but
now that seed will be the first new
tree again. I can't believe we did it!

Then the President gave me a medal.
"Oh wow, I've got a medal, I thought,
it's really big and heavy too. But then

he gave everyone getting off the space shuttle one and it was to weigh us down so we wouldn't float away in the low gravity.

"Pluto welcomes the Fisher family!" the President suddenly bellowed in a superhumanly loud voice, and then I realised he was using a megaphone. "Let the light show begin!"

He pressed a button and a single light high up in the dome ceiling fizzled and went pop.

boing

pop

pop

fizz

"That was our welcome light show," the President said, looking embarrassed. "It needs some work."

I saw Dad's eyes light up (pun) as he saw something to fix and soon he and the President were well away chatting about sprangs and sproings and stuff like that.

"Let's go and get a Whirlywang," said Straxi. So we did.

Jon

P.S. We went to see the seed. It's a tree!!!

Class 5H

Northcroft School

England

Earth

Tuesday 8 August 2317

Dear Jon,

How interesting to hear about your lovely welcome to

Pluto. It would be even more interesting if I could

also read your essay about Pluto's geography that I

asked for. Please include it with your next letter.

Best wishes,

Mrs Hall

Vertigo Hotel

Dome 1

Pluto

Fiveday 11 Armstrong 2317

Dear Mrs Hall,

Straxi's family had a welcome party for us in Doolyboppers which is their café.

This is Straxi's mum. She makes all the food in Doolyboppers like Blobble Burgers, Ri Tentacles and Whirlywangs. I asked her if she had always wanted to be a chef and she said no, when she was

little she wanted to be a snargler. A
snargler is a blind double-ended slug thing
that lives in the Pulsating Swamp. Luckily
she changed her mind and became a
chef.

This is Straxi's dad. He
serves the food and is
known for his weird hairstyle.
He also made all the giant plastic models
of food that are stuck on the roof. His
ambition is to build a giant Whirlywang
that can be seen for miles around. So
far he has dug the foundations.

Bryd is Straxi's twin. I wouldn't mind having a twin, but if big bruv had been a twin I would not have survived this long.

We helped Straxi's mum make Whirlywangs which is their most popular dessert and famous. This is how you make them:

1. Get a weird-shaped vase. Straxi's mum has loads just for serving Whirlywangs.

2. Pour in a cup of smick flour and a

pinch of boggleplops. Mix them together.
If you are Straxi, throw some smick
flour at Bryd.

3. Pour over some gorgelicker juice. It
sticks to the smick. It also sticks to
Bryd's face.

4. Throw on the yuffs. Straxi likes to
do it from a distance. Bryd places each
one carefully in the perfect position.
This is a good way to tell Straxi and Bryd
apart if you are not sure.

5. Put on some more yuffs. Put one up

Bryd's nose.

6. Take a long spoon, dip it in tinglepowder and stick it in the top. Or if you are Bryd, throw it at Straxi.

7. Say sorry and clean up the kitchen.

8. Eat Whirlywangs.

Jon.

Class 5H

Northcroft School

England

Earth

Tuesday 15 August 2317

Dear Jon,

I enjoyed hearing about how to make Whirlywangs,
and if I had smick flower, boggleplops, gorgelicker
and yuffs I would certainly try making my own.
However I really would like to see your essay on
Pluto's geography. Or I have some lovely quadratic
equations I can send you instead.

Best wishes,

Mrs Hall

Vertigo Hotel

Dome 1

Pluto

Fiveday 18 Armstrong 2317

Dear Mrs Hall,

Here is my essay. I wrote it sitting in
Doolyboppers so it might have bits of
Blobble Burger stuck to it.

Straxi said we should watch the sunset
as it was going to be special tonight and
in our honour. The sunsets are really
just the President switching off the lights
at bedtime as the sun is seven and a

half billion kilometres away so it
might as well not be there.

When there is a special occasion
the President programs in
a really nice sunset and
everyone makes sure they
watch.

The sunset started and I was really
excited but all that happened was the
sky turned the colour of sick and then
went black.

I said maybe the President was sick of

us already just like Captain Timothy
Peake XII was on the journey here, but
Straxi said the dome lights haven't been
working properly for ages and sometimes
it's dim all day, just like big bruv.

Jon

day

night

sunset

sick

GEOGRAPHY ON PLUTO by Jon Fisher

Pluto is really cold and icy with lots of frozen gasses and winters that last over two hundred years. ✓ What a nightmare place you might think, but you are wrong because the people who arrived here first quickly built a nice warm dome and filled it with plants so they could breathe. ✓

I am sure there is not a Yeti on Pluto (note to self: check this).

When you look out of the domes you see huge great mountains of ice, but you would die if you went out there, so never go mountaineering on Pluto.

Inside the domes there are lots of interesting places called zones which were designed by people who won competitions set by the President. ✓ Like here in Dome 1 there is the Blue Prairies which were designed for nature and the Glowing Canyon which was designed for people to stand around and take photos. Then there's the Pulsating Swamp which went wrong but was built anyway and is popular with snargler spotters.

Lots of things on Pluto have gone wrong it turns out, like vomblefruit and sunsets, but the President says that is what makes it so special and you learn by your mistakes. *I agree.* ✓ Good job he thinks that as he was the one who had the bright idea of spraying the whole planet with Vom-Be-Gone to get rid of the smelly vomblefruit trees. But I didn't remind him of that because I expect he feels bad enough.

Now there's not just one dome but lots with different landscapes in them and the President wants to build even more domes with even more zones.

"Will you be holding another competition?" I asked, but he said the experience with the Pulsating Swamp had put him off.

I am sending you a stone from the Glowing Canyon. Straxi collects them but she has two like this already. And another fifty that are slightly different. The President has asked her to stop as otherwise they will have to change the maps to show the Glowing Canyon in her bedroom instead. Plus it is too bright for Bryd to get to sleep.

Interesting, Jon! Remember you are the President's guest so try to be polite.

Class 5H

Northcroft School

England

Earth

Tuesday 22 August 2317

Dear Jon,

Thank you for the stone. It is rather heavy, but will

be a useful source of heat in the classroom this

winter, providing it doesn't burn a hole through the

show-and-tell table before then.

If there is anything else LIGHT you can send, this

will make a marvellous display.

For your next piece of homework I would like you to

write about the jobs people do on Pluto.

Best wishes,

Mrs Hall

Too late!

To do:
✔ Mark Rex Smith's homework
✔ Buy more red pens
✔ Water class cactus or buy replacement
✔ Fix show and tell table

Vertigo Hotel

Dome 1

Pluto

Fiveday 25 Armstrong 2317

Dear Mrs Hall,

We are staying at the Vertigo Hotel
which is a <u>very</u> tall building specially
made for the thousands of tourists they
expected to come to Pluto.

Gran is the only other person there.
Maybe when the lights are working and
the sky is not the colour of
sick it will help.

We have the top floor with our own
bedrooms and a huge living room
looking out over all the domes. I can
actually see Doolyboppers from here!
Straxi is going to get one of the giant
plastic yuffs to flash so we can signal to
each other.

Straxi and Bryd go back to school soon.
They go in the mornings and have the
afternoons off. They can do whatever
they want in the afternoons as long as
they write about it in their homework
book and show the teacher they have
learned something. Straxi is showing

she's learning about blue-headed
skwitches. She measured one but it
kept moving and then it flew off with the
tape measure and ate it. Can we do
that? Have the afternoons off school, I
mean, <u>not</u> fly off with tape measures
and eat them.

Here is some homework. It's not really
<u>home</u>work though. It's Plutowork.

Jon

JOBS ON PLUTO by Jon Fisher

There are lots of jobs on Pluto as it is a challenge to survive. But even here they still have...

TEACHERS

Straxi's gran is the head teacher of Straxi's school which is called Flumpenslurp Blurble School and is named after the first person to arrive on Pluto from Earth. ✔I wouldn't like being called Flumpenslurp Blurble, but I like someone else being called it.

When Straxi's gran gets home from school she takes out her plain earrings and puts in some big colourful flowery ones so everyone knows she's Home Gran now not Teacher Gran. But every so often when Straxi and Bryd throw yuffs at each other she threatens to take them off again and become Teacher Gran.✔

DOME CLEANERS

These people make sure the dome is clean. ✓ Doesn't sound very exciting, does it? Well it is as they get to squirt **giant** hoses at the sky to clean the roof and sides of the dome. Sometimes they squirt the hoses at each other. I would like to be a dome cleaner.

GRAVITY GUYS

These people make sure no one floats away. They sell heavy clothes in shops and give out heavy medals if they see you floating in the street. ✓ If you want to float you can go to a gravity party in a special tent. There you will see all the Gravity Guys flying about doing stunts because they love it really.

FRIENDLY FOLK

Friendly Folk are exactly that - your friends. They walk around making sure no one is lonely ✓ and that people have help with shopping and stuff. ✔ They also put on fun events. They wear jackets with FF on them so you know they are helping you and not just stealing your groceries.

GUARDIANS

They are like the police but on foot and on Pluto. They aim to be with you in five minutes. ✔ They are often out of breath. Their motto is, 'With you in five!' but the older ones take ten.

That is five different jobs on Pluto but there are many more just like we have on Earth except we don't have Swamp Guides or Skwitch Herders or Pluffs. At least I don't think we do.

No we don't – or do we?
(Note to self: check)

Good essay, Jon.

To do:
✔ *Arrange meeting with Head re Rex Smith*
✔ *Replace class cactus ASAP*
✔ *Get some flowery earrings for home*

Class 5H

Northcroft School

England

Earth

Tuesday 29 August 2317

Dear Jon,

I thought you might like to see the poster for my

Bring Back Handwriting campaign with you as my

Ambassador of Handwriting. I am having it turned

into a hologram and beamed to every school in the

country. Isn't that wonderful? You must be so

proud.

Best wishes,

Mrs Hall

Vertigo Hotel

Dome 1

Pluto

Happyday 2 Sacagawea 2317

Dear Mrs Hall and 6H,

Your poster has arrived. It is in big
bruv's hotel room with a ~~mus~~ moustache
drawn on it. I hope he adds a beard as
well so no-one recognises me. Is it too
late to stop being
your Ambassador of
Handwriting? All I did
was write some letters
to Pluto.

Jon Fisher wants
YOU
to get WRITING!
☐ + ◊ + ? = ⬠

Today we went with Straxi's family to visit the Pulsating Swamp, famous for being full of snarglers. It was the same day as the Annual Snargler Count (a big event in the snargler spotters' calendar) so to get in and see the swamp we had to join the Snargler Spotters' Society.

Big bruv wasn't happy about that as you have to wear an anorak with 'I love snarglers' on it, but me, Straxi and Bryd thought they were quite cool. Also they keep the swamp from getting on your clothes so big bruv

wore one after all. We all put on high

boots and waded into the swamp.

All of us except Straxi's gran. Turns out

she had her own <u>special</u> boots as she is

a member of the Secret Snargler

Spotters' Society, the society for people

who secretly like snarglers. She even

has her own anorak with 'I secretly love

snarglers' on it.

"Not that secret then," I said, but she

said she normally only puts it on after

dark. "Classic mad Gran,"

Straxi whispered.

"Is there a <u>Secret</u> Secret Snargler
Spotters' Society for people who
secretly like the Secret Snargler
Spotters' Society?" I asked, getting my
tongue in a twist, but Mum said don't be
silly which I thought was rich as she had
a snargler on her head at the time.

Straxi got a certificate for
spotting the most snarglers
ever in a single session and
is now a Gold member
of the Snargler Spotters' Society.
Thirteen was more than enough for me.
Anyway, I was busy taking photos of big

bruv's back with a snargler on it so I can send it to his girlfriend. Ha ha!

Jon

PS Rex Smith would make a <u>brilliant</u> Ambassador for Handwriting.

Thank you

for participating in our annual Snargler Count!

Record the number of snarglers you spot on the chart below for a chance to win free Gold Membership of our Snargler Spotters' Society!

How many snarglers did you spot?

Name	Snarglers spotted
Dad	4
Mum	0
Straxi's mum	5
Straxi's dad	8
Big bruv	1
Little sis	3
Jon	13
Bryd	22
Straxi	135

Class 6H

Northcroft School

England

Earth

Tuesday 5 September 2317

Dear Jon,

Rex Smith would not make a brilliant Ambassador

for Handwriting. Ha ha!

Rex smith

I have told you before not to write on other people's

letters or posters, Rex. Since you kindly signed your

name I have no qualms in deducting a merit.

Remember Smith should have a capital s.

Anyway it is far too late to make any changes. My

campaign to bring back handwriting is getting so much support that we have been able to get funding to display the poster on ten-foot-high e-billboards across the solar system. Fabulous!

6H are very excited about our class project and especially snarglers, so now we would like to know more about animals on Pluto. Please send me an essay on the wildlife of Pluto.

Please do not send me a snargler.

Best wishes,

Mrs Hall

To do:

- ✓ Ask office to check Jon's post for snarglers
- ✓ Explain to office what snargler is – picture? Not sausage
- ✓ Prepare shoebox with breathing holes for emergency snargler capture

Vertigo Hotel

Dome 1

Pluto

Happyday 9 Sacagawea

Dear Mrs Hall and 6H,

A weird thing happened today.

Gran asked me to go for a walk with her
around the Glowing Canyon as the
skwitches in town keep trying to steal her
handbag and yesterday they flew off with
someone's shopping.

"Maybe they will take big bruv," I said,

hopefully. I haven't seen very much of
Gran as she spends most of the time
having romantic meals with the President
or wowing people with her somersaults at
low gravity parties.

Anyway, we took some dark glasses
from the box provided to protect our
eyes from the glow and as we walked
Gran talked about all the different
adventures she's had planet-hopping
since Grandad died.

The most dangerous one was being
chased by a blarb-ringed flapper while

Ta da!

Yeah!

hello
earth

Woo-hoo!

surfing on Neptune and we laughed as she remembered being almost torn to shreds by its **horrific fangs.**

"Well," she said, taking off her dark glasses, flinching and hurriedly putting them back on again, "now I'm about to go on the greatest adventure of all."

"Brilliant, you're going to get revenge on the blarb-ringed flapper at last!" I said.

"Not yet. Maybe next year," she said.

"But what I mean is I'm going to marry the President of Pluto."

"Oh," I said. It didn't sound very adventurous to me. I asked her if she would need any special equipment, like when she went to Neptune she hired an anti-matter powered surfboard, but she said no.

All she needed was to make sure I understood she still loved Grandad as much as ever but it was time to move on to the next adventure.

Then she asked me what my favourite memory of Grandad was and I said it was when he took his false teeth out and

turned them upside down without them leaving his mouth.

We both enjoyed that thought for a while, and then I said, "When you've got married will you get revenge on the blarb-ringed flapper then?" And Gran said <u>yes</u> and a dangerous glint came into her eye.

Here is my Plutowork. Is my

face really on ten-foot-high e-billboards?
If so, I do not want to come home.

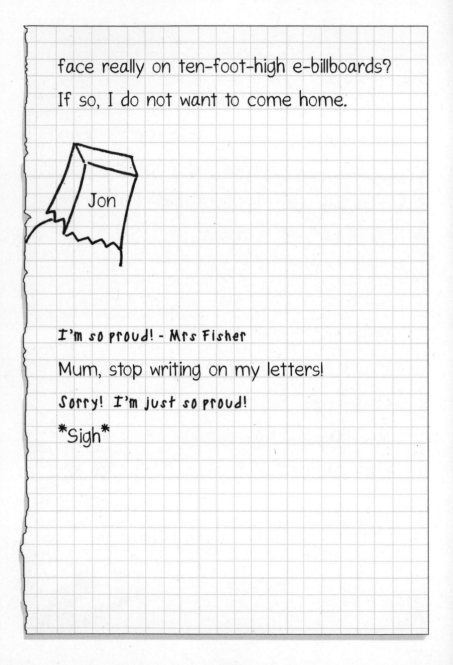

Jon

I'm so proud! - Mrs Fisher

Mum, stop writing on my letters!

Sorry! I'm just so proud!

Sigh

THE WEIRD AND WONDERFUL WILDLIFE OF PLUTO by Jon Fisher

Animals on Pluto are very strange due to lighter gravity and freak accidents. ✓ When the first settlers (Flumpenslurp Blurble and her friends) got here, they brought animals from Earth but some of the animals escaped and ate strange algae and breathed strange air. ✓ Luckily they were all rescued but as more animals were born they all got more weird until they turned into the creatures you see today.

"Why didn't the humans go weird as well?" I asked Straxi and she just pointed at her dad and raised her eyebrows so I guess she means they did.

BLUE-HEADED SKWITCHES
You see these giant birds everywhere. ✓ In fact it is one

person's job in Dome 1 to keep them off the roads and stop them playing with people's shoelaces. Straxi would like to be that person when she is older.

Skwitches are ten feet high so all you see are legs like giant uncooked spaghetti walking around, unless you look up or the skwitch looks down. They aren't very clever but Straxi says they are deep thinkers. ✓ Skwitches have nowhere to make their nests now as all the vomblefruit trees were sprayed and died apart from one. ✓ Instead of collecting branches they have been collecting handbags, so maybe they have

something else in mind. Straxi is planning to follow one and be the first person to find out. She has put food on the roof of Doolyboppers to attract them and has made herself a skwitch costume as a disguise.

PIMPAMS

Pimpams are like large flat erasers
with faces on one end. They ripple
about making soft noises. Sometimes they are kept
as pets. ✔ You can stroke them if you see them in the
wild or on a wall but you have to pretend you aren't
going to or they get scared.

ZORKS

Zorks are like bean bags with an eye on a stalk.
They don't do a lot except make you feel very
uncomfortable. "Stop watching me!" you might say to
a zork, but they will just blink and carry on staring at
you until you can't bear it any more and have to walk
quickly away. ✔

SNARGLERS

Enough has been written about these ✔ — I mean, what
else is there to say? They float about in swamps and

people in anoraks count them. I've done it myself
and still don't understand why.

BIG BRUVS *Not really an animal.*
(Or is he? Check.)

One of these weird and dangerous animals has
recently been spotted on Pluto. They luuuurve
their girlfriend like a big soppy wet sponge but will
attack anyone else, especially if you barge in on
them in the bathroom when they are squeezing their
massive yucky red spots. Avoid.

Thank you for not sending a snargler, Jon.

(Note — recycle shoebox or use for dead cactus.)

Class 6H

Northcroft School

England

Earth

Tuesday 12 September 2317

Dear Jon,

It was most interesting for 6H (and myself) to learn

about animal life on Pluto. We have been making

pimpams from kitchen roll tubes, zorks from

beanbags and snarglers from old socks. We have not

made a 'big bruv' and from my memories of his school

days here I think that is wise.

The classroom smells terrible from all the old socks

but I told 6H the smell would be much worse if there

were thirty real snarglers on the display table.

I am extremely pleased with how my handwriting
poster campaign is going. I even saw you on the side
of the town hall the other day.

Big head!!! RS

I have now been invited to visit other schools and I
will be encouraging them to write to penpals on
different planets just like we do.

Best wishes,

Mrs Hall

Rex Smith, I know that was you.
Minus one merit. And you should
not use multiple exclamation marks.
One is much more effective!

kitchen roll

bean bag

old sock

Vertigo Hotel

Dome 1

Pluto

Fiveday 15 Sacagawea

Dear Mrs Hall and 6H,

Today I visited Flumpenslurp Blurble
School where Straxi and Bryd go. It's
really small as there aren't many children
on Pluto yet and the teachers do other
jobs in the afternoon, for
example Mrs Urdlepun is a
plumber.

I had to give a talk to the <u>whole</u> school

called 'Life on Earth'. I was given <u>ten</u> minutes. "Tell the children what it's like living on the mother planet," said Straxi's gran who is the head teacher and had her Teacher Gran earrings in to prove it.

I stood there panicking as my mind filled with tractors and doughnuts and sharks and ten-pin bowling and all the other things on Earth and they all jumbled together and made my knees go shaky.

But then Straxi stood up and gave me all the letters I had written to her about big

bruv and little sis and you getting us to
write to each other and tomato sauce on
the ceiling and I read them out and
everyone laughed and I think they
enjoyed it after all.

Jon

Class 6H

Northcroft School

England

Earth

Tuesday 19 September 2317

Dear Jon,

How wonderful that you read out your letters in front
of the whole school! It sounds like a lovely place to
learn. I mentioned your idea of having afternoons off
to Mr Cooper and he said he would love to have more
time to work on his golf swing but he feared the
school governors would say otherwise.

Mrs Hall

To do:

✓ Order fire extinguisher for glowing rock
✓ Find Rex Smith's doodle of Mr Cooper and
destroy ASAP

Vertigo Hotel

Dome 1

Pluto

Fiveday 22 Sacagawea

Dear Mrs Hall and 6H,

We can't find little sis.

What happened was we were all walking down Main Street on the way to Doolyboppers as Straxi's mum was going to try out a new recipe called Ving Wibbler Surprise. The surprise is that ving wibblers aren't <u>actually</u> as bad as you think, even though they look and smell disgusting.

Anyway, we never got to Doolyboppers as
I heard a **scream** and little sis
was being lifted into the air by a skwitch
which was holding on to the back of her
dress with its beak. The scream was
from Mum and when she stopped we
could hear little sis singing a happy song
as she was carried away out of sight.

Mum panicked, Dad panicked and even
me and big bruv panicked although we
tried to look like
we weren't,

and then Gran who has been here longer than us and knows what to do on Pluto said, "I will call honeybun - I mean, the President."

They don't have mobile phones on Pluto so she spoke into a microphone on a stick at the side of the pavement and about five minutes later a Pluto Guardian ran up looking out of breath and said she would call the President.

Then she spoke into the microphone and another five minutes later the President ran up. He was <u>really</u> out of breath so we all told him what had happened while he tried to get his breath back. Then he said one at a time and asked me to go first as Gran told him I write things down so I must be observant and notice stuff.

So now the President has lots of Guardians and Friendly Folk searching for little sis. He said don't worry as Pluto is very safe and she can't get out of Dome 1, but he has ordered a net to be put over the Pulsating Swamp just in case.

Jon

Class 6H

Northcroft School

England

Earth

Tuesday 26 September 2317

Dear Jon,

I am sorry to hear your little sister is missing.

Remember, Pluto is a very safe and friendly place

compared to Earth. I can't understand why more

people don't go there – oh yes, it's seven and a half

billion kilometres away.

Anyway, skwitches sound like very nice birds and

Guardians and Friendly Folk sound like very nice

people. I am sure they will find her soon.

Here are some posters made by your little sister's class.
The likenesses aren't exact but I hope they help you
find her. Good luck and please let me know what
happens. All of us at Northcroft School are thinking
of you.

Best wishes,

Mrs Hall

MISSING

LITTLE SIS

Description: small and smiley

Hairstyle: My Ickle Pickle Dress Up Princess Pony

Likes: ponies, kittens and glitter

If found bring to <u>Doolyboppers Café</u> where Straxi's mum says you can have free whirlywangs for a year with as many yuffs as you like.

Vertigo Hotel

Dome 1

Pluto

Happyday 30 Sacagawea

Dear Mrs Hall and 6H,

Little sis must be **really** hungry and
thirsty by now but she's <u>still</u> not back.

I have put the posters up with one of
mine and we are going on another

search. Straxi has
made us both skwitch
costumes so we can
blend in with the herd

and find out more about where they go.

I don't want to dress up as a skwitch but I don't want to not get little sis back either even though she does make me play My Ickle Pickle Dress Up Princess Pony and brush my mane with a sparkly brush.

So I will.

Jon

CUNNING PLAN TO FIND LITTLE SIS

By Straxi Dooly, assisted by Jon Fisher

1. Straxi to put on skwitch costume made by Straxi Dooly. Must look very convincing.

2. Jon to dress as old lady with handbag.

What??!! I thought I was a skwitch too? Jon please don't write on my cunning plan. Skwitches are stealing handbags. We are setting a trap.

But why do <u>I</u> have to dress as an old lady??

OK, you can just be yourself carrying

Gran's big flowery purple handbag and
everyone will know it's you.

All right. Let's just get this over with.

I will if you'll let me get on with the plan!

3. Skwitch flies down and steals
handbag. Jon holds on to handbag.
Straxi holds on to Jon. Skwitch flies
off with Straxi and Jon. Hang on

4. Skwitch takes us to little sis.

This is insane.

Thought of anything better?   No.

Then let's go.

Class 6H

Northcroft School

England

Earth

Tuesday 3 October 2317

Dear Jon,

I was somewhat concerned to read your plan. Please
write and let me know that you are safe and have
not been carried off by a skwitch like your little sister.

Yours anxiously,

Mrs Hall

To do:
✓ send this ASAP
✓ Water new cactus, or replace

Class 6H

Northcroft School

England

Earth

Tuesday 10 October 2317

Dear Jon,

I fear you have been taken by the skwitches as well.
6H are very worried.

I'm not! Rex Smith

Apart from Rex Smith. We are all waiting to hear
from you. Please send us a note to let us know where
you are.

Yours really anxiously,

Mrs Hall

Skwitch Nest

Top of Dome 1

Pluto

Dear Bryd,

This is Straxi. HELP! We've been
carried off by a skwitch! My plan
worked but now we are STUCK!

What happened was that Jon dressed
up as an old lady with a handbag.
I didn't want to. She made me
Anyway, a skwitch grabbed the
handbag. We both held on tight and
the next minute we were flying through

the air. The skwitch flew up and up until we reached the top of the dome where the lights are. It's full of skwitch nests! They must have dragged their old nests up here when the vomblefruit trees got sprayed. So no wonder the lights aren't working.

It dropped us in a nest and guess who was in the nest next to us? Jon's little sis! She is quite happy as the nests are lovely and warm. We opened Gran's handbag which is all we have and threw her some boiled sweets.

Finally she caught one and it was her
favourite as well.

I am going to tie this note to the
skwitch's leg and hope it flies back to
Doolyboppers and drops the note by the
front door. So when you read it get
help but don't get it too soon as I'd like
a bit longer up here first but Jon
doesn't.

Straxi

Skwitch Nest

Top of Dome 1

Pluto

Dear Bryd,

It's Jon this time.

We think Straxi's note must have fallen

off the skwitch's leg as no one has

come. Or it didn't get to Doolyboppers.

Please put some skwitch food out to

attract it. Straxi says try ving wibblers.

They are the closest thing to vomblefruit.

We are in a skwitch's nest at the highest point of the dome ceiling. We can see the whole of Dome 1 from here — even the Blue Prairies and the Glowing Canyon. Unfortunately we can also see the Pulsating Swamp.

Straxi is pleased no one's come to rescue us but I'm getting hungry as we have run out of boiled sweets and dropped most of them. When you get this **please** can you strap two Blobble Burgers to the skwitch's leg before it flies back.

Little sis has made friends with her skwitch and brushes its feathers with her sparkly hairbrush.

She has called it Fiona the Feathery Pony.

Jon

Skwitch Nest

Top of Dome 1

Pluto

Dear Bryd,

This is Straxi. The Blobble Burgers didn't
arrive so I guess you didn't get Jon's
note either. It's getting dark so the
skwitch is settling down next to us in
the nest and won't be flying over
Doolyboppers until tomorrow.

It looks very comfortable with its long
legs hanging over the side which Jon
says makes it look like it's on the toilet.

We have called it
Armitage Shanks.

The orange and red
sunset lights are
coming on but all
they are lighting up is
the skwitch nests because there is a
nest on top of every single one. Ours is
orange. Jon looks like a
tangerine. I am tying this note
to Armitage Shanks's leg. Jon
is adding something as well.

Straxi

Jon Fisher's Last Will and Testament

To Mum, Dad and my next of kin
(whatever that means).

I may never see you again, so here are
my instructions in case I do not return.

1.   Big bruv is **not** to have my room.
It will become a *museum* where
people can go if they want to pay their
respects and think about all the
amazing things I did like saving
life on Pluto and becoming a skwitch.

2.   Big bruv is not to touch <u>any</u> of my stuff. It will be part of the museum and sacred.

3.   My GIANT FACE is to be removed from Mrs Hall's handwriting posters as a mark of respect.

4.   My school lunch box is jammed behind the radiator in the PE changing rooms. I hereby leave it and its contents, whatever state they may be in, to

Rex Smith

of 6H.

Skwitch Nest

Top of Dome 1

Pluto

Day 2 of captivity

Dear Mr President of Pluto,

We (Straxi Dooly and Jon Fisher) are
writing this letter to you as we have
been kidnapped by skwitches.

It's all right for me as I want to be a
skwitch when I grow up, but Jon
doesn't, plus he is still dressed as an old
lady and wants to change as his tights
are itching. We are getting hungry and

(S.S.S.)

dream of Whirlywangs.

The skwitches have been building their nests on the lights and that is why it has been so dim, like Jon's big brother, and there have been no decent sunsets or sunrises for ages and they are the colour of sick.

We are writing to ask you if you can build the skwitches a proper place to make their nests. Then we will have lights in the dome again but also the skwitches will be able to make better nests and have babies and not kidnap people and handbags because they are confused.

We would be confused too if you took our home away.

Straxi Dooly and Jon Fisher

MISSING

ONE ANNOYING BROTHER.

REWARD FOR NON-RETURN:
EVERYTHING I OWN

I can't believe you wrote this. Get out there
and search for him. Now! - Mum

Skwitch Nest

Top of Dome 1

Pluto

Day 3 of captivity

Dear Mum, Dad and the other one,

I don't think you or Bryd or the
President are getting any of our letters.
Maybe they are falling off the skwitch on
the way down and getting delivered to
people who couldn't care less like the
Pluto
equivalent of
Rex Smith.

We are getting worried as tomorrow is Dome Cleaning day and those hoses they aim at the roof are powerful.

Straxi says she has a plan. This letter is in case her plan goes wrong. Our plan. No, this is definitely your plan, Straxi.

My last wish is that my face be removed from Mrs Hall's handwriting poster. A dying wish has to be obeyed.

In memory of the noble skwitch

Straxi would like a statue of a sad

skwitch in the town square next to the

one of Flumpenslurp Blurble's spaceship.

Wish us luck,

Jon

PS The plan involves Fiona the Feathery

Pony and Armitage Shanks.

PPS We are going to ride them back

to Doolyboppers.

PPPS What could possibly

go wrong...

Flumpenslurp Blurble School

Dome 1

Pluto

Threeday 11 Earhart 2317

Dear Mrs Hall,

My name is Mrs Urdlepun, Straxi Dooly's class teacher. I just wanted to let you know in writing that Jon and Straxi and Jon's little sister are safe and sound.

The whole of Dome 1 has been looking for them, but no one thought to look up. That is, until two skwitches came flying down towards Doolyboppers café at top speed.

One landed elegantly on the front lawn and Straxi and Jon's little sister climbed off with big grins on their faces. The other crashed into a giant plastic yuff on the side of the building.

Luckily I was leading 6U past on a class outing so we were able to help, and after a few minutes of pulling we were able to get Jon's foot out of the middle of the O of Doolyboppers. He popped out like a cork from a bottle of furgel juice and we all fell in a big heap. 6U said it was the best outing they'd ever had.

Keep up the good work with your handwriting campaign.

Kind regards,

Urma Urdlepun, teacher and plumber

PS I have enjoyed writing this letter. If you
agree perhaps we could exchange letters on a
regular basis and learn more about each other's
teaching methods. I also have some interesting
knitting patterns to share.

Vertigo Hotel

Dome 1

Pluto

I'M ALIVE!

Fiveday 13 Earhart

Dear Mrs Hall and 6H,

Sorry you haven't heard from me for ages. It's not my fault. A skwitch ate my homework.

Little sis and Straxi and I got swiped by skwitches and had to live in their nests at the top of the dome which is like a big fake sky. Straxi wanted to stay there forever but I said, "Think of all the

Whirlywangs you'll never get to eat," so she came up with a plan.

The plan was to ride our skwitch, Armitage Shanks, and little sis's skwitch, Fiona the Feathery Pony, all the way back down to Doolyboppers.

Little sis jumped onto Fiona and as she flew past us Straxi leapt on too which I thought was amazing, and then she said, "Come on scaredy pants!" which wasn't so amazing so I grabbed

Armitage's feathers and we were off.

On the way down I learned a lot about skwitches. The main thing I learned is that skwitches don't like to be ridden.

"Eek! Argh! Gah!" I yelled, which to a skwitch probably means, "Lovely day isn't it?" but what I actually meant was, "Look out, you're heading towards a giant plastic yuff and we're going to die."

Luckily we bounced onto the letters spelling out Doolyboppers above the café door. After taking some photos and a short video, Straxi's class helped me down and the skwitch flew off with a small satisfied smile on its beak.

They are cleverer than you think.

Jon

Class 6H

Northcroft School

England

Earth

Tuesday 17 October 2317

Dear Jon,

What an eventful few weeks you have had! I think I

will set you one of my favourite pieces of work - What

I Did On My Holiday. It will make a lovely addition

to our Pluto display table. About six sides should be

enough.

Best wishes,

Mrs Hall

Vertigo Hotel

Dome 1

Pluto

Fiveday 20 Earhart

Dear Mrs Hall and 6H,

The President has launched a new
competition to design some sculptures
for the skwitches to nest in while they
wait for the vomblefruit tree to grow.

Straxi's dad is already sketching out his
designs. I hope the skwitches like
modern art.

Dad has got his wish and is helping to fix the lights. He is actually quite good at fixing things, although he prefers taking them apart really. He has promised an amazing sunset tonight. We shall see.

And Mum is busy helping make the Doolyboppers garden nice again after the skwitches trampled it. So it looks like we might be staying a bit longer.

Little sis is happy wherever she is, especially now Feathery Fiona is her best friend.

And as for big bruv, I caught him sneaking out of the door in an 'I secretly love snarglers' anorak. He was going to a Secret Snargler Spotters' meeting!— He claimed he was only going because Straxi's gran had asked him to.

"Why have you already got the anorak then?" I asked, and he threw it at me but missed and it landed on some tomato sauce on the table and he had to wear it anyway. I <u>love</u> it here.

Jon

Class 6H

Northcroft School

England

Earth

Tuesday 24 October 2317

Dear Jon,

What a lovely letter and how heart-warming to see
your whole family has embraced the Pluto
community spirit! Just to remind you of the
homework I set – What I Did On My Holidays. I
look forward to reading it.

Best wishes,

Mrs Hall

Class 6H

Northcroft School

England

Earth

Tuesday 31 October 2317

Dear Jon,

Are you getting my letters? Did you see the

homework you are supposed to be doing? Jon? Jon!

Mrs Hall

_To do:_
✓ Buy new cactus – fake one?
✓ Detention with Rex Smith
✓ Book tickets for trip

Class 6H

Northcroft School

England

Earth

Tuesday 7 November 2317

Dear Jon,

Don't worry about sending your homework. I am
coming to Pluto to visit Mrs Urdlepun and can
collect it in person.

See you very soon,

Mrs Hall

Vertigo Hotel

Dome 1

Pluto

Twoday 14 Norgay

Dear Mrs Hall,

You can't come to Pluto.

The skwitches have gone mad and are attacking everyone, especially teachers.

No — the snarglers have crawled out of the swamp and are on the rampage.

No, it's worse. Anyone who writes letters is <u>banned</u> from Pluto. ~~Hang on, that means I can't send you this letter.~~

Forget all that. It's just a really, really <u>bad idea</u> to come to Pluto.

You would **hate** it.

I mean, everyone dresses <u>so</u> weirdly, and the food has got weird names and even weirder tastes, the animals are crazy, the weather is always like spring and everyone wants to be your friend, and if

you're a tourist you get treated like a
celebrity — it's **terrible** really, you'd
hate it so please, <u>please</u> — don't come
to Pluto.

Mum's just told me to stop writing as
we're going to meet your space shuttle.

I've got a bad feeling about this...

Jon

STAY AWAY

DOME 1 UNDER ATTACK!!!!

Jon

I've found a zork in the back garden!
I'm going to follow it and
blend in with the herd.
Meet me at Doolyboppers
in ten minutes. I've made
you a zork costume!

Straxi

THE SOLAR TIMES

Pluto edition

Max 26C, min 9C 16th Earhart 2317 1 plound

REMINDER

Gravity medals or weighted clothes must be worn at all times, unless you are attending a gravity party. If you're floating and you didn't mean to, see the Gravity Guys for more medals.

PLUTO HAS LIGHT!

It looks like Pluto residents will finally be able to see each other again - the mystery of the dodgy dome lights has been solved. After Jon Fisher and Straxi Dooly were 'bird-napped' by blue-headed skwitches, they discovered that the pesky giant birds have been making their homes up in the lights. "It's very cosy and warm up there," said Straxi. "I definitely still want to be a skwitch." Jon, who is on holiday here from Earth, said the experience had not put him off Pluto. "I don't mind if something like that happens again, so long as I'm not dressed as an old woman this time."

The President was quick to respond to the discovery, launching a competition to design new nesting places for the birds while they wait for the vomblefruit tree to grow. "To celebrate, I am working on producing the best sunset ever this Happyday," he promised. "I just have to press the right buttons in the right order."

See page 2 for the competition winner.

GRAVITY PARTY

This Funday in Blurble Park. Learn how to do the latest crazy moves! Guest-starring Granny Fisher.

FOOD & CULTURE

Have you tried ving wibblers? Don't be afraid, they're really not that bad ～ Ursula Copperbottom, author of ～mblefruit Cookbook.

WEATHER

Next week will be comfortably warm with a short evening shower, as voted for by Meteor Street residents. The next street to vote for the weather will be Canyon Street.
See page 5 for more details.

COMPETITION WINNER:

Mr Dooly for his post-modern ambient sculptures that communicate what it is to be feathered in the modern age, plus voted most comfortable by skwitches.

JOB VACANCIES:

We're recruiting Pluffs! Find out more about this important job at the Pluff Open Day in the Town Hall.
No Pluffing experience required!

Can you cope with one or even two visitors a year? Then why not work in the Pluto tourist office?
This is a part-time role.

FRIENDLY FOLK NEEDED!

Do you fancy becoming one of Pluto's Friendly Folk? We spoke to Boogle Bopton to find out what it's like.

"Being Friendly Folk is great," says Boogle. "You never know what you'll be doing next. Unless you haven't got anything to do. Then you pick up litter. But you never know what you're going to pick up, so that's great too."

Boogle says he was chosen for the job because of his cheerfulness. "I like to brighten up people's day. If someone looks lonely I'll go and chat to them. If they look annoyed I'll move on."

We asked Boogle what has been the most unusual task he's been asked to do?
"Once I had to queue for someone in Doolyboppers while she did her shopping," he said. "I got to the front of the queue and she still hadn't come back, so I ate her Whirlywang. Whirlywangs, actually. There were three."

Was the customer angry? "No, she didn't have time to eat them either."

If you'd like to become a member of the Friendly Folk, just ask one when you see them.

The End

Look at it now!!!

Gran's engagement ring

Armitage Shanks!

Little sis and her best friend

MONTHS OF THE YEAR ON PLUTO

January - Gagarin
Yuri Gagarin from Russia was the first man in space and orbited the Earth in his bubble-shaped spaceship in 1961.

I'm having a ball in here!

VOSTOK

I'd be a lot faster if I could use both feet...

February - Fiennes
Sir Ranulph Fiennes is one of the greatest living explorers and was the first person to cross Antarctica on foot.

March - Mukherjee
Bimal Mukherjee was an Indian cyclist who cycled round the world. It took eleven years!

This bike was the latest model when I started!

Does my head look big in this?

April - Aldrin
American Buzz Aldrin took part in the first ever moon landing in 1969.

May - McArthur
Dame Ellen McArthur broke the record for the fastest solo person to sail round the world in a yacht.

June - Johnson
Amy Johnson was the first woman to fly solo from England to Australia in 1929.

July - Grylls
Bear Grylls is a British adventurer and survival specialist.

August - Armstrong
Neil Armstrong was the first man to walk on the moon in 1969.

September - Sacagawea
Sacagawea was a Native American kidnapped from her tribe, who became part of an expedition exploring the American West in the eighteenth century.

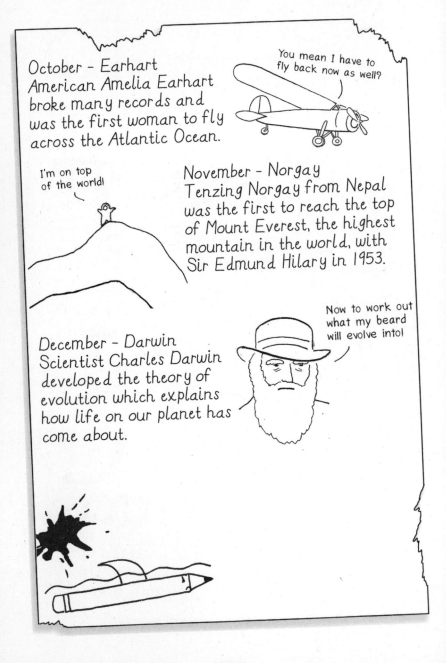

October - Earhart
American Amelia Earhart broke many records and was the first woman to fly across the Atlantic Ocean.

You mean I have to fly back now as well?

I'm on top of the world!

November - Norgay
Tenzing Norgay from Nepal was the first to reach the top of Mount Everest, the highest mountain in the world, with Sir Edmund Hilary in 1953.

Now to work out what my beard will evolve into!

December - Darwin
Scientist Charles Darwin developed the theory of evolution which explains how life on our planet has come about.

DO **<u>YOU</u>** HAVE WHAT IT TAKES TO BE ...

PRESIDENT
of PLUTO?

The President is looking for someone to take his place while he goes on his honeymoon to Saturn, and is holding a new competition.

If you think you're the one for the job, pick up a form at the Tourist Office and apply today!

Good luck!

To do:
✓ Enter competition

ENTRY FORM

NAME *Mrs Marion Hall*

HOME PLANET *Earth*

OCCUPATION *Teacher*

I want to be President of Pluto for a month because:

Ooh now, let me see... Running a planet must be very similar to running a school. We will have assemblies every morning in the town square, compulsory spelling tests for all, merit marks of course, school dinners with lots of cabbage and I will bring the class cactus. Plus I could get everyone on Pluto writing letters to penpals! Oh dear, I'm running out of room - I have so many wonderful ideas -

Send to Pluto Tourist Office, Lowell Road, Pluto